Jake the Snake

Written by
Jill Atkins

Illustrated by
Claudia Souza

Ransom

By the side of a big fishing lake
there was an old viper called Jake.
He got his fang stuck
in a deep pile of muck.
He was really a silly old snake.

In the lake were a drake and a duck.
They could see Jake had run out of luck.
The duck said, "Can I help?"
as Jake started to yelp.
"We will help get your trapped fang unstuck."

They sent for a dentist called Dave
who was always forgetting to shave.
He came to the lake
took a good look at Jake
and said, "You must try to be brave."

Dave called to the duck and the drake,
"We must jump so we make the fang shake."
Then the duck said, "Quack, quack!"
as she jumped on Jake's back
and Jake said, "I've had all I can take!"

"It's no good," said the dentist called Dave.
"This long fang is not easy to save.
I'm sorry old mate
but we left it too late."
As he went off he gave them a wave.

Then a girl who was fishing said, "Quick!
I think this will help do the trick.
Take some of my line.
It's a very fine twine.
We'll pull out that fang in a tick."

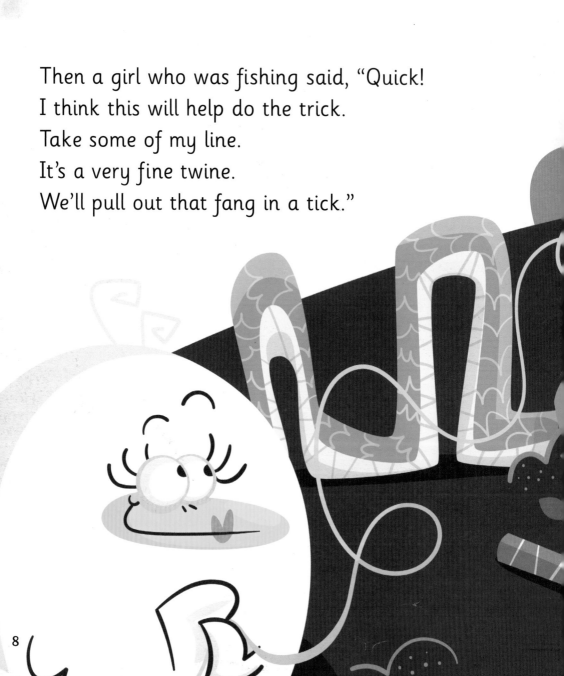

So they stood at the lake side by side.
When they pulled hard, they felt their feet
    slide.
Jake yelled, "Stop! Just hold back!
You are making a crack,
and that crack has become very wide!"

Jake's face was as pale as can be
when he saw that his fang was in three.
He said, "What a shame.
You can all take the blame,
but I'm glad that at last I am free."

They stuck the three bits with some tape
and they made such a very odd shape
that Jake's friends had to smile.
The fang stuck out a mile
and poor Jake could do nothing but gape.

So Jake soon became very thin
with his food spilled all over his chin.
But he got over that
and became very fat,
so he had to shift out of his skin!

Now Jake is a happy old snake.
He lives with his friends at the lake.
His fang has been mended.
This tale is now ended,
of duck, drake and silly snake, Jake.